Gertrude
the Goose who Forgot

JOANNA and PAUL GALDONE

FRANKLIN WATTS, INC.
NEW YORK, 1975

ertrude Goose was all set to go shopping in town...
But the key to her house was nowhere to be found.
"Oh my, oh me! Oh, where can it be?
I forget where I left my rusty old key."

"Now let me just sit
and think for awhile."
So she sat and she thought.
Then she rose with a smile.

"Oh ginder, oh gander, how silly of me,
Now I know what I did with that rusty old key.
I should have it right back any minute now,
'Cause I left it next door with Big Bossie Cow."

"Big Bossie, Big Bossie, how silly of me,
  Have you seen what I did with my rusty old key?"

"Of your key," said Big Bossie, "I've seen not a sign,
  But this hat must be yours. It's surely not mine!"

"My hat, my hat! Oh what a surprise!
  It's the one that keeps falling over my eyes."

"Oh ginder, oh gander, how silly of me,
Now I know where I left that rusty old key.
It's right over there at the paddock, of course,
Where I ate golden grain with Rushmore the Horse."

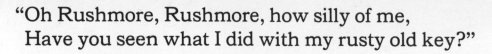

"Oh Rushmore, Rushmore, how silly of me,
Have you seen what I did with my rusty old key?"

"Of your key," said tall Rushmore, "I've seen not a sign,
But this shawl must be yours. It's surely not mine!"

"My shawl, my shawl! Oh this is great!
Now I *must* find my key so I won't be late."

'Oh ginder, oh gander, how silly of me,
Now I know what I did with that rusty old key.
It's there in the sty where I stopped to dig
With my wonderful friend, Old Curlpink the Pig."

"Oh Curlpink, Curlpink, how silly of me!
  Have *you* seen what I did with my rusty old key?"

"Of your key," said fat Curlpink, "I've seen not a sign,
  But these socks must be yours. They're surely not mine!"

"My socks, my socks! Now how can it be?
  I was sure they were home where they ought to be."

"Oh ginder, oh gander, how silly of me,
  Now I know where I left my rusty old key.
  It's there in the garden by the old wheelbarrow,
  Where I found some good seeds with Teedaweet Sparrow."

"Teedaweet, Teedaweet, how silly of me,
Have *you* seen what I did with my rusty old key?"

"Of your key," chirped Teedaweet, "I've seen not a sign,
But these shoes must be yours. They're surely not mine!"

"My shoes, my shoes! What a wonderful sight!
They're my only pair that fit me just right!"

"Oh ginder, oh gander, how silly of me.
Now I know what I did with that rusty old key!
It's still in the barn near Purmeece the Cat,
I dropped it there once when she pounced on a rat."

"Purmeece, Purmeece, how silly of me,
  But have *you* seen what I did with my old house key?"

"Of your key," grinned Purmeece, "I've seen not a sign.
  But this bag must be yours. It's surely not mine!"

"My bag, my bag! That I take when I shop.
  Will this forgetting of mine ever stop?"

"Oh ginder, oh gander, how silly of me,
Now I *know* where I'll find my rusty old key!
I lost it last evening when Digwell the Dog
Showed me his bones buried under the log."

"Oh Digwell, Digwell, how silly of me,
But have *you* seen what I did with my rusty house key?"

"Of your key," yawned Digwell, "I've seen not a sign.
But this fan must be yours. It's surely not mine!"

"My fan, my fan! That I use when I'm hot.
But my rusty old house key it surely is not!"

"Oh ginder, oh gander, how plumb dumb of me.
My hope's running out for finding that key!"
So she walked sadly home till she met the Gander.
"You look lovely today," said her friend Alexander.

"Oh Alex, I've looked all around for my key,
'Cause I can't lock my house without it, you see.
I've searched every place, but it's just as I've feared,
My rusty old key has plain disappeared."

"That *is* a shame, Gertrude. Now here's what I'll do,
I'll go back to your house and look once for you."

When they got to her house Alex glanced at the door.
"Silly Gertrude, you don't have to look any more!"

"My key, oh, my key!
 You're a wonderful friend!
 Now...just *where* is that party
 I'm dressed up to attend?"

SBN 531-02735-X
LC 73-19583